Meredith Nicholson

Short Flights

Meredith Nicholson

Short Flights

ISBN/EAN: 9783337250447

Printed in Europe, USA, Canada, Australia, Japan

Cover: Foto ©Andreas Hilbeck / pixelio.de

More available books at **www.hansebooks.com**

SHORT FLIGHTS

BY

MEREDITH NICHOLSON

———

With a weak, uncertain wing
And a short flight, faltering
Like a heart afraid to sing.

———

INDIANAPOLIS
THE BOWEN–MERRILL CO
1891

CONTENTS

SONNETS

SHORT FLIGHTS

TO THE SEASONS.

SEASONS *that pass me by in varied mood,*
  As on the impressionable land you leave a trace,
    Molding sometime a delicate flower's sweet face,
Touching again with green the somber wood,
Or drawing all beneath a snowy hood,—
    Am I not worthy as they to have a place
    In your remembrance? Am I made too base
To know what weed and thorn have understood?

Fair vernal time, I need your quickening
    Even as the sleeping Earth!   O summer heat
Make flower and fruit in me that I may bring
    Full hands to Autumn when above me beat
      The serious winds; and Winter, make me strong
      Like the glad music of your battle song!

SAT EST VIXISSE.

I.

To have lived!
To have felt a quickened beat
    Of the heart in spring;
To have known that something sweet
    Moved the birds to sing;
To have seen dim waves of heat
O'er a field of green retreat!

II.

To have found the hiding-place
    Of the wild wood rose;
To have held, a little space,
Any flower that grows;
To have known a moment's grace
Looking in a loved one's face
        To have lived, to have lived!

III.

Still, doth it suffice alone
    That the world is fair?
O'er what fields have these hands sown?
    Are they gold or bare?
And though all the flowers are flown,
If to God my heart is known,
Then shall I in truth be shown
    How to live, why to live!

SONG.

G LAD and sad make rhyme, my dear,
  Glad and sad make rhyme.
Though the sun may not appear,
    Though there be a time
When the hours are very long,
    And there is no joy for you,
Weave this thought into a song:
    Glad and sad make jingle true—
        Happy jingle true!

They are joined together, dear,
    Joined together they,
Like the dark sky and the clear
    Of an April day.
Like the grief that dies in gladness
    Turmoil into peace will grow,
Soon there is an end of sadness—
    Glad and sad make rhyme, you know,
        Perfect rhyme, you know,

They make perfect rhyme, my dear,
Perfect as can be;
Falling sweet upon the ear,
Telling you and me
That the thorn and rose are wed,
That night holds in store the dawn,
And till hope and trust are dead
Glad and sad will jingle on,
Jingle, jingle on!

'TIS NEVER NIGHT IN LOVE'S DOMAIN.

'TWAS morning when one found his way
   Within the garden lands of love.
He lingered till he thought the day
Should surely unto night yield sway,
   But morning's sun still shone above
In skies unmarred by evening's gray,
      While on the air rang this refrain—
      'Tis never night in love's domain.

Love's palace beauteous is, and tall,
   And broad, and grand is his estate,
Gay courtiers throng each spacious hall
Where laughing echoes ceaseless fall
   And mock the silent outcast, hate,
Who ever cowers by post and wall,
      And scowls as rings the glad refrain—
      'Tis never night in love's domain.

And thence through groves with myrtle grown
    He followed Venus' dove-drawn car
By paths he ne'er before had known,
And yet, the morning had not flown,
    And yet, fresh winds blew from afar
As came, in ne'er decreasing tone,
        The song through which ran this refrain—
        'Tis never night in love's domain.

Ah, love of mine, how well we know
    The glories of those garden lands
Through which Lethean waters flow!
Oft we have wandered to and fro
    Down those bright halls, and seen the hands
Of tiny elves that beckoned so
        They kept the time to this refrain—
        'Tis never night in love's domain.

ESTRANGED.

I T was but yesterday that thou
  Wert with love-whispers eloquent,
Yet come and look upon her now
   That life is spent.

How strangely white the face hath grown,
  No longer prest by kisses fond;
Why turn'st, now that her soul hath flown
   And rests beyond?

Why enter'st not the darkened room
  To touch again those cold, white lips—
So cold and white, seen in the gloom
   Of Death's eclipse?

Thou wert so loving once, but now
  Take that cold hand as lovers may,
Imprint a kiss on that calm brow,
   Nor turn away.

It was but yesterday that thou
  Wert with love-whispers eloquent—
Thou wilt not look upon her now
   That life is spent.

WHEN FRIENDS ARE PARTED.

TIME keeps no measure when true friends are parted,—
    No record day by day;
The sands move not for those who, loyal-hearted,
    Friendship's firm laws obey.

It is not well to note with dull precision
    The flight of days or years;
Memory depends not on a proof by vision,
    And has no foolish fears.

The migrant birds when they are Southward flying
    Have no regrets; they go
Full of the knowledge born of faith undying,
    That they again shall know

The homes and nests which they have left behind them
    Unmarred by change the while;
The Southern lands they seek will but remind them
    Of the North's summer smile.

And so I know that you will come to meet me
    In the old, well-loved way;
That, though a year go by, you still will greet me
    As kindly as to-day.

WHEREAWAY.

WHERE are you going my bright blue eyes,
　　My boy so happy-hearted?
You are very young and very wise,
　　And early you have started.
Where is the city you're bound for, lad?
　　Come tell me of it truly;
Is it one that is fair, and one that is glad
　　And was it builded newly?
Oh, tell me whereaway my lad—
　　　　Whereaway?

The day is fair and the skies are blue,
　　Come rest awhile and listen:
By far too great is the world for you,
　　The spires in dreams that glisten
Are far away from this quiet place
　　With many a mile between,
So rest, blue eyes, for a little space
　　Here where the slopes are green—
Oh, tell me whereaway my lad—
　　　　Whereaway?

Oh, dim and vague is the early haze
       That holds your world of seeming;
This day is fairer than other days
       Only in boyish dreaming,—
So do not hasten but pause to tell
       Why you make such a hurry—
Do you want to go, have you pondered well
       About the cost and worry?
Oh, tell me whereaway my lad—
       Whereaway?

Oh, dear blue eyes and brave young heart
       Why must you turn to leave me?
Am I so old that we now must part,
       Why will you go to grieve me?
But he turns away with a smile and nod
       And will not tell me truly
About the place to which he will plod,
       If old or builded newly;
He does not answer "Where, my lad?"
       Whereaway?

A SECRET.

H E said, "No one shall ever learn
This secret that my heart must keep;
No matter how the words may burn,
No matter how my heart may leap,
No one shall know I love her so,
No one shall know, no one shall know!"

But though his lips were tightly sealed,
The very birds his secret guessed,
For in his eyes it was revealed,
And in his face it was confessed—
"I love her so, I love her so,
But none shall know, but none shall know?"

The wind soon found it and ran on
To tell it to the wondering flowers,
And bear it to the gates of dawn,
Where loiter all the coming hours,
That they might know he loved her so,
That they might know, that they might know!

Some time all secrets must unfold,
  And soon did he a listener seek,
To whom his story might be told
  Before the laughing world should speak
    And tell her (if she did not know!)
    He loved her so, he loved her so!

DISAPPOINTMENT.

THE broad-armed wave that reaches for the land
    Sees not the towering rock that bars the way
Unto the longed-for play-ground of the strand,
      Until, thrown back, it sees through tears of spray.

STRIVING.

IT is not much that I can do,
 My hands are weak,
The lines they draw seem never true;
 The works I speak
  Are not the ones I long to say,—
  I speak not prayers I long to pray.

It is no coward spirit, no—
 I try to learn
How others bravely strive and go
 Rewards to earn,
  And yet success is never mine—
  I labor on a false design.

They are not much, these little things
 That form my task,
Yet constant seeking never brings
 What I would ask,
  And of what use is life to one
  Who never knew a victory won?

But this one thing I know, that He
      Who guides the stars
Will look in charity on me
      And see the scars
           Which show that I have tried to trace
           A path that weeds could not efface.

AN IDOLATER.

I READ of pagan priests in idols hiding,
      That with their own lips they might make reply
To prayers of worshippers in them confiding—
          To vouchsafe or deny.

And all idolatry has not departed;
      For yet I faith in one fair idol hold,
Unlike those of the heathen, hollow-hearted,
          Voiceless, inert and cold;

But one who dwells, a queen, among the living,
      Whose eyes light up, my waiting eyes to greet
And speak, before the lips, sweet answer giving
          From her soul's judgment seat.

LOVE'S MIDAS TOUCH.

YOUR love has made life dear to me;
  Until you came I did not know
How beautiful the world could be—
  How full of joy its days could grow.

Once peace was not in anything,
  But love has made life dear to me;
The winter has given way to spring,
  And skies are fair and clear to me.

My heart is listening when you speak;
To hold your hand or touch your cheek,—
Since love has made life dear to me!
Sends flying love and fear through me.

Glad is the grass your feet have pressed,
  Your eyes throw joy on all they see,
Around you there is gracious rest,
  Your love has made life dear to me.

IN ETHER SPACES.

SOMEWHERE in space there is a realm where lingers
    Each word that ever fell from lips of man,
All music stirred to life by touch of fingers,
        All sounds since time began.

Rumble of quaking earth and plains upturning
    Creation morn; the sullen beat of rain,
The coo of dove with olive-leaf returning,
        The stir of life again.

A Child's soft treble in the temple, heeded
    By doctors who about him listening drew;
"Father, forgive them," on dark Calvary pleaded,
        "They know not what they do."

The songs are there which echoed through dim ages,
    And chants of kneeling priests at pagan shrines,
The speech of prophets writ on history's pages
        In God-directed lines.

There dormant dwells the roar of battle royal,
  The clash of arms amid war's furnace flame,
Victorious cries of warriors brave and loyal,
      A people's loud acclaim;

With words that gladdened hearts of earliest lovers,
  And curses since night's robes trailed Eden's sky,
While vague as half-remembered dreams there hovers
      Each mother's lullaby.

O sounds afar in ether spaces dwelling,
  In mighty minstrelsy awake! Unite
In chords the story of the æons telling
      Since stars first gemmed the night.

MY PADDLE GLEAMED.

MY paddle gleamed, the light canoe
  The river's waters glided through
  With scarce a sound to fret the air;
 The sun shone bright, the morn was fair
And from the South soft breezes blew.

O'erhead the swallows darting flew,
  Then dropt to earth to brush the dew
   From off the tangled grasses there,
   My paddle gleamed!

In form as perfect, fresh and new
As when they first in Eden grew
  God's gifts, before, lay everywhere;
  Behind, the city's toil and care;
Content, I joy's full measure knew—
  My paddle gleamed!

FAITHLESS.

A H, yes! Thy love was like the stars, but not
      Like faithful stars which gleam with steadfast light,
But as a darting ærolite, swift shot
      Across the blackness of a sombre night,
Fading as quickly, and as soon forgot.

GRAPE BLOOM.

I WALK 'mid vines which rest upon
   An arbor o'er a garden way
   Where southern breezes come to play
And never-ending races run.

The dew drips from the clustering vines,
   A swallow like a shuttle cleaves
   The air above and vainly weaves
His fancies into unseen lines.

But stealing forth and dwelling there
   Within the shadows of the walk,
   A perfume comes as when gods talk
And their glad breathings fill the air.

Scarce seen among the vines the shapes
   That hold and throw the rare perfume—
   The tiny bits of early bloom
Presageful of the coming grapes.

And when they ripened grace the vine,
   That sweetness shall return again,
   Like hopes fulfilled to trustful men,
And have new life in autumn's wine.

ILL-STARRED.

OH, prayers and sympathetic tears
    For each and every ill-starred knight
For whom ring no victorious cheers;
    For those who, early in the fight,
    Saw daylight turning into night
And yielded up to Fate their spears.

The dented shield, the pierced cuirass,
    Sad story is it that they tell
Of brave young knights whose hopes, alas!
    Bore meagre fruit; who fighting fell
    Before the foe they could not quell;
Who found no wine within the glass.

For some there are but ill-equipped
    To face the world; some weak of will
And soon faint-hearted, feeble-lipped,
    Fit but the lowest posts to fill,
    Some shivering with the coward's chill,
And of the armor "courage" stripped.

Oh, you 'gainst whom the fates are set,
 E'en though you've failed on every field
To gain fair honor's banneret,
 Let high above be held each shield,
 Each one with purpose strong annealed,
And all shall win a victory yet.

THE SOLDIER HEART.

ONE day in careless wise I said:
"They were no heroes, they who bled
To save the Nation and to free the slave;
There is no honor now in being brave;"
And thought not how my father hearing me—
(He who had fought with Sherman to the sea,
True as a knight of storied chivalry),
Would feel the sting my words conveyed, as though
I deemed the venture of his life should go
A thing unworthy of remembrance.   Then
His look of pain (soft are the hearts of men!)
Made me think deeply of the soldier's part,
(As when on Memory's day the quick tears start
To see the line each spring becoming less,
The slowing step, heads' winter snowiness!)
And vowed I then that while my blood should run
I should not be a son
To speak a word not kindly of a soldier true;
To utter naught but praise of all who dared to do,
Whether in mail of gray or clad in honest blue!

He who cares not
That his sire fought;
He who shall think not proudly of the days
His father felt the blaze
Of war's red furnace flame against his cheek,
Has but a coward's heart, too poor and weak
To throw the blood through faltering limb—
Earth has no place for him!

While there is hearth and home to save,
'Tis something to be brave—
'Tis something to have ventured near to Death,
And felt his chilling breath!

AN UNWRITTEN LETTER.

S HE wrote a letter with her eyes,
  Well-filled with words of bliss;
Then, like a prudent maid and wise,
  She sealed it with a kiss.

MY LADY OF THE GOLDEN HEART.

M Y lady of the golden heart, she comes each day
      Down by the lodge-gate that I keep; she comes de-
    murely,
And her two hounds sedate do follow and obey
      Her slightest wish, and they do love my lady surely.

She comes each day, my lady of the golden heart,
      Sometimes a-riding or sometimes she comes a-walking;
The birds along the hedge they do not even start
      When she comes by, sometimes to her big hounds a-talking.

"Good morrow" says my lady, (she whose heart is gold),
      And gold out of her heart makes bright the gateway;
The sunshine of her face in winter time does hold
      Green meadows and sweet flowers and makes a summer
    straightway.

My lady, she whose heart is gold, my lady goes
      Each day into the village, bread and good wine bearing
To those that sick be, and my gentle lady knows
      All of the village folk and for them she be caring.

Now as she comes each day,(gold is my lady's heart),
 Or goes away upon some errand Heaven has sent her,
The gates of my poor heart, they do fly far apart,
 But there my lady fair and sweet, she will not enter.

DREAMS.

LIKE shadow-freighted ships which softly creep
  Across some far-off ghostly main,
  They haunt the chambers of the brain,
And kiss their fingers to the watchman, Sleep!

CARDINAL NEWMAN.

" To the last I never recognized the hold I had over young
men."—Apologia pro Vita Sua.

NO more the sun may know the strength it hath
    To stir the bark in spring with quickening blood:
No more a storm controlleth its great wrath,
    Or doleth out the measure of its flood!

There is a quality of lasting youth
    That knoweth not the force that gave it birth;
Some souls God pointeth subtler ways of truth,
    As highest tribute to their lasting worth.

He hath in souls like thine deposited
    A quenchless flame as calm and strong as dawn;
Across the world thy potent fire is shed,
    Born of the "kindly light" that leadeth on!

ON THE MEDITERRANEAN.

THE GREEK GIRL'S SONG.

TO-DAY my lover tends his flocks;
   He roams with them through fragrant meads,
And guides across the barren rocks;
   With his own hands the lambs he feeds,
And soothes them when the winds are cold
Or terror comes among the fold.
  They soon forget the night's alarms
  When folded in his shielding arms.

     So good and true to them is he
     I know he will be kind to me.

My lover walks in paths of peace,
   He would avoid the conflict's noise
And bid the warring legions cease.
   He is content with simple joys;
He fain would always journey through
Tall grasses shining in the dew
   And tend his sheep and dream his dreams
   Beside the quiet mountain streams;

So faithful is his love of home
His heart I know can never roam.

—

THE SHEPHERD'S SONG.

As fair as the flocks that graze
There 'gainst the hill's restful side;
As sweet as the breath of night
When across dim flowery ways
Pours a mellifluous tide,
Winging an odorous flight:

Thus is the maiden who sends
Songs to the shepherd who tends
Sheep by the streams, and who dies
In the delight of her eyes.

Down by the shore in the night
Rush the great breakers, nor cease
Oft till the dawn lights the crest;
And so is love in its might,
Stirring my soul from its peace,
Leaving the shepherd no rest.

Oh, if the sheep could but learn
For me the answer I yearn!
Come, my fair flock, we shall see
What is the answer for me!

WATCHING THE WORLD GO BY.

S WIFT as a meteor and as quickly gone
   A train of cars darts swiftly through the night;
Scorning the wood and field it hurries on,
         A thing of wrathful might.

There, from a farmer's home a woman's eyes,
      Roused by the sudden jar and passing flare,
Follow the speeding phantom till it dies,—
         An echo on the air.

Narrow the life that always has been hers
      The evening brings a longing to her breast;
Deep in her heart some aspiration stirs
    ﹅   And mocks her soul's unrest.

Her tasks are mean and endless as the days,
      And sometimes love cannot repay all things;
An instrument that rudely touched obeys
         Becomes discordant strings.

The train that followed in the headlight's glare,
  Bound for the city and a larger world,
Made emphasis of her poor life of care
  As from her sight it whirled.

Thus from all lonely hearts the great earth rolls,
  Indifferent though one woman grieve and die,
Along its iron track are many souls
  That watch the world go by.

RIGHTEOUS WRATH.

HOW splendid is the righteous wrath
    Born in a good man's soul!
Ignoble things fly from his path,
    Loud thunders round him roll,—
Yet tenderness and love he hath.

Like some gigantic forest fire,
    His mighty anger sweeps;
An eager flame of awful ire,
    At every wrong it leaps,—
Still, lasting peace he doth desire.

Then, swift as flies the meteor's spark,
    His anger disappears;
Born for the hour it met its mark,—
    He sootheth now love's fears,
While wrong sits trembling in the dark!

SUNSET.

TWO giants meet upon the hills
  And one is day, the other night;
The trees draw near, the sky leans down
  To watch their test of might.

I cannot see them struggling there,
  But soon I know that one is dead,
For lo! the trees and hills and sky
  Are suddenly splashed with red!

RONDEAU OF EVENTIDE.

A T eventide when we are prest
 By shadows and seek any rest
  That twilight brings at waning day,
  Ah, well with us if we can say
For aye we sought and found the best.

God's hand all nature has caressed
Till beauty is his love confessed,
  Till bud and bloom his love display
    Through eventide.

Why should we not pursue our quest
For such good things as bear the test
  The things worth loving bear alway?
  "Full life, full life," we sometimes pray,
Full life to higher life addressed,
    Till eventide!

A PRINCE'S TREASURE.

[To His·Royal Highness, Russell Fortune.]

O UR little prince can't understand
     That this is one of many springs;
He thinks these days for him are planned,
     And that for him the robin sings.

All wonder-eyed he walks afield
     And makes an invoice of the joys
     God strews around for little boys,
And thinks for him they're first revealed.

It is a solemn thing to him!
     He wonders if it's right to pull
     The little wild flowers beautiful
That in the sea of grasses swim.

More gentle than the violet,
     He studies o'er those eyes of blue—
Blue as his eyes are brown, and wet
     As *his*, sometimes, are wet with dew!

Appreciative eyes are his!
    Into his apron takes he all
    The flowers that to his hand may fall—
The poorest weed so precious is!

His feet leave but the vaguest hints
    Of steps along the shadows where
    The knightly trees bend down and swear
Allegiance to their little prince.

O gentle, princely lad of ours,
    May nature ever hold your heart,
    And knowledge of her ways impart
Through lessons of the spring-time flowers;

May spring itself pass ever on
    And never lead to summer's dust,
But make your life an endless dawn,
    With endless love, and faith, and trust!

DIEU VOUS GARDE.

MAY Allah in thy heart unfold
Perpetual-blooming roses;
May His sweet peace to thee increase
Until the evening closes.

And may tall palms before thee rise,
Hot sand to gardens turning;
May dates and wine be always thine,
Amid the desert's burning.

Let enemies be put to flight,
Before thy spear uplifted,
And may thy way be as a day
From starry vistas drifted.

Oh, Allah watches through the night,
His trustful children viewing;
His love is deep, but he will keep
Renewing and renewing.

SWEETHEART TIME.

I

IT is a time before the rose
    Has blossomed to its form complete;
Before the hidden fragrance knows
    How rare it is, and sweet.

A time it is when hearts are light,
    And shadows are a thing as far
Away as darkness from the sight
    Of evening's brightest star.

There is an undertone of song
    Vague, like the mists of early day;
An undertone that steals along,
    Forever far away.

II.

The walls that guard King Love's fair home
    Are tall and strong; yet cannot hold
From those who by the gateway roam
    Some share of hoarded gold.

So youth and maiden wandering near
    In straying beams of light are caught.
Their eyes serene know not the tear
      Through fuller loving wrought.

It lasts for just a little while;
    It is love's playtime, one brief hour
With tender sighing to beguile—
      A bud before the flower;

It is a time before the rose
    Attains its fairest form complete;
Before the subtle fragrance knows
      How rare it is, and sweet.

THE ROAD TO HAPPINESS.

HERE'S the path our feet shall press
    To the land of happiness;
There are guide-posts by the way
That we may not go astray;
Spots there are where we may rest,
Of King Happiness the guest;
Basking in the sunshine's glow,
While the joyous pilgrims go
Ever onward to the gates
Where the Queen of Joy awaits
Those recruits her king shall gain
On the way to his domain.

Such a joyous army this!
Banners leaping for a kiss
From the winds that sweep along
Bearing songs that well belong
To a road whose glory lies
Always under sunny skies.

By this road no toll gate stands
With its ever-barring hands,
Yet of every passing soul
There is asked a certain toll.
It is this—that we shall share,
As we tread the thoroughfare,
All we have with those who lose
What they gain, or who refuse
To accept what is bestowed
By the master of the road.

What a simple engineer
Marked this path! It is so clear
That to miss it is to turn
And its cooling shadows spurn.

Any road our feet may press
Is a road to happiness,
And that land is anywhere
That we turn away from care
To the army of a king
Who is ever journeying
To the city, by whose gates,
His fair queen of Joy awaits.

GUARDING SHADOWS.

G RIM watchmen are the jealous trees
    Above their moon-born shadows—Thus
May foolish men guard mysteries
    Which they have made mysterious.

ART'S LESSON.

O glorious marble statue,
   What gain I looking at you?
Your beauty is so old,
You are a form so cold
I can not understand you
Nor feel for him who planned you.
I easier lessons seek
Than those in chiseled Greek.

I turn to you my fragrant;
Bedewed and straggling vagrant,
You are a simple flower,
And scarce live out the hour
Here in the garden by-way
(That still is Nature's highway!)
Yet utter from the grass
Lessons from Phidias!

IN THE SHADOW.

I WOULD not have thee otherwise,
        O cloudy skies;
I would not change the night to day
        Nor drive away
The shadows that are hanging o'er
        My hearth and door.

There is some good that lurketh where
        The lightnings flare;
There is a peace that bideth in
        The fiercest din;
A vernal light doth look upon
        Fields winter-won.

If God were not the Overheart,
        Nor had a part
In all the wounds that hurt us so!
        But He doth know
And doth in patience see and bless
        In gentleness.

How sturdy and how great, O earth!
Within thy girth
Thou wieldst what passion and what pain
O'er man's domain;
And yet within thy shadows blest
Is perfect rest.

Turn not unto the light too long
Friend, with thy song!
Thou hast not need to look afar
For hill or star;
Here in the shadow rest is found
Deep and profound.

"LEAD, KINDLY LIGHT."

"LEAD, kindly light," I heard the glad bells ring,
      And thought how God existeth everywhere.
'Twas in a city strange that, sweetest thing!
"Lead, kindly light," I heard the glad bells ring,
And Summer stole into the early spring,
      For where the kind light leadeth all is fair.
"Lead, kindly light," I heard the glad bells ring,
      And thought how God existeth everywhere.

SONGS AND WORDS.

I.

THE songs you sing, the songs you sing,
     They are such songs as need not words,
They are the songs that soar and ring
     Like utterance of wildwood birds.
The ear is puzzled at the sound—
     They are so far from common art
That what is best in them is found
     By simply listening with the heart!

II.

The words you speak, the words you speak,
     Have little of philosophy;
They voice not things that wise men seek,
     They have no hint of poetry,
And yet each syllable that slips
     Up from your soul and bubbles o'er
The yielding gateway of your lips
     A gracious meaning holds in store.

III.

The songs you sing are simple songs,
    Your words are words that children use
To tell of love, complain of wrongs;
    You may the guiding notes confuse,
(If any notes e'er met your eyes!)
    They rise, and live, and lingering,
Each song and word alternate dies
    In words you speak, in songs you sing.

FOR A NEW YEAR'S MORN.

L IKE some tired reader who has put aside
    His book a little while, sick of the tale,
Careless a moment how the plot may run,
Indifferent to the part he has perused,
Then with new interest going back to find
How fared it with the story's people, so
Here at the gate of this new year I stand.
Weary we grew long since, my Comrade soul!
So tired we are of all our eyes have found,
So strong our yearning for new sights and sounds!
Yet on this morn the world is fair again,—
Ah, very fair, and full of light and joy;
And holding forth new hope that comes of faith,
And adding to our faith that lies in God.
Now, like some traveler in a desert lost,
Straining his eyes across the wastes of sand,
Then, sudden, finding tracks but freshly made
That give new courage to the wanderer,—
So now, my Comrade soul, we turn away
From dreary wastes, we see the tracks that show
Where others have gone on and found the way
As we can find it. Come, old Comrade,—friend!
Give me your hand, we must march on again!

THREE FRIENDS.

[Paul Hamilton Hayne, Sidney Lanier and Robert Burns Wilson]

THREE noble friends the South has given me,
  Two biding now beyond the farthest gate,
  One living still, great-hearted, soul elate,
From trammeling passions free.

The twain now unbeholden to our eyes,
    Were soldiers for a cause they thought was right—
    They were such men as set the torch alight
That marks our destinies;

Yet, with a song that rings above the din
    Of battle, and with brows where there might rest
    The victor's crown, or singer's wreath, more blest,
Through hymns of peace to win.

I read one morning, in a day long gone,
    The songs of Hayne, all odorous of the pines;
    The heart of Nature throbbed along the lines—
Her joy was in his dawn.

The hills and streams to him were never dumb,
>They gave their secrets to his own heart's keeping;
>Grand music in the oaks and pines was sleeping
Waiting for him to come!

And you, Lanier, cut down like some tall tree
>By an insidious foe—upright and strong
>Until the last, and with your parting song
From Deathland floating free!

Sweet dawns were‾yours, bright noons and starry nights;
>Your heart lay on the bosoms of the hills—
>Clear was your soul as dew that God distills
Upon His sacred heights!

And you are gone, and only one remains
>Of the three Southern singers loved so well;
>To-night the wind in sympathy would quell
The grief of woods and plains—

Saying: "They were our friends, they understood
>The messages we spoke into their ears;
>Now they have passed beyond our hopes and fears
Unto a higher Good."

But he who still is here, he well has caught
        The spirit that is Nature's, and is hers
        Only for her most loved interpreters—
Ah, nobly he has wrought!

And Southern winds that to the northward roam,
        And misty stars that shine above us dim,
        Each evening bring me utterance of him
To my far Northern home!

A RHYME OF LITTLE GIRLS.

PRITIIE tell me, don't you think
   Little girls are dearest
With their cheeks of tempting pink,
   And their eyes the clearest?
      Don't you know that they are best
      And of all the loveliest?

Of all girls with roguish ways
   They are surely truest;
Sunshine gleams through all their days,
   They see skies the bluest,
      And they wear a diadem
      Summer has bestowed on them.

Lydia doesn't care a cent
   For the newest dances;
She is not on flirting bent,
   Has no killing glances,
      But without the slightest art
      She has captured many a heart.

Older sisters cut you dead,
    Little sisters never;
They don't giggle when they've said
    Something very clever,—
        They just get behind a chair,
        Frowning, smiling at you there.

Florence, Lydia, Margaret
    Or a gentle Mary,
They form friendships that, once set,
    Never more can vary,—
        Stanch young friends they are and true
        Always clinging close to you.

Buds must into blossoms blow,
    (Morn so early leaves us!)
Maids must into women grow,
    (There's the thing that grieves us!)
        Psyche knots of flying curls,
        That's good-bye to little girls!

THE BATTLES GRANDSIRE MISSED.

C OME, boy, and sit upon my knee,
 And turn to me your eyes,
That I, down in their depths may see
 A hint of those blue skies
 Beneath which once my father fought
 (Your grandsire! and I am not old!)
What time our banner's stars were caught
 In treason's eager hold.

A boy, as you are now a boy,
 I did not understand
That traitors could their flag destroy
 And cut in twain their land;
I heard the tramp of marching men,
 So long ago that seems!
You can not know what times were then
 Though you may guess, in dreams.

And then my father went away;
 How would it be if I
Should leave you, boy of mine, to-day—
 Should leave you and should die?

Your eyes are wet; O closer come!
      There is no more of war;
Peace long has shown that there are some
      Kind things to struggle for.

You "wonder whether grandpa got
      In all the fights?" Well, lad,
It was Bull Run where he was shot,
      The first big fight they had!
But let us, you and I, insist
      That this of him be said:
The only battles that he missed
      Were fought when he was dead.

"He would have fought, had he been there?"
      You ask of me, my child;
He never would have ceased to dare
      Those who our flag defiled.
And always, in the spring, keep tryst
      With Memory by the head
Of one who not a battle missed
      Except when he was dead.

BARRED.

ONE cheerless night when winter winds were sowing
    Over the world their cold, white seeds of snow,
While from my window pane the fire was throwing
    Taunts to the elements with its bright glow,

A poor, storm-driven bird, its lost way winging,
    Paused when it saw the flame's reflected light;
Unto the window for a moment clinging,
    Then downward fell, forever lost to sight.

And so it is, I thought, that poor hearts yearning
    For more of life, charmed by its outward sheen,
Must backward fall, the truth too quickly learning,
    That death, cold and unyielding, stands between.

A SLUMBER SONG.

BABY, you stand by a gate that leads
        Into a land of dreams;
There's a drowsy watchman here who heeds
        Never the straggling gleams
Of light that stray from the far-off sun—
Always for him it's twilight begun—
                And we stand by the gate,
                And watch and wait,
                And watch—and wait!

Little one, hear what the stream sings of,
        Here in this quiet land;
It sings of the joy of mother love—
        Sings to birds in the sand—
To the strange, tall birds with dreamy eyes,
That look at you, dear, in mute surprise,
                While we stand by the gate,
                And watch and wait,
                And watch—and wait!

If you open the gate, no one will know;
    The guard will never guess.
You must open it gently, slowly—so!
    No one has heard, unless
Those dreamful birds, or the dreamland sheep,
Heard you stealing through their land of sleep
        While I stood by the gate,
        To watch and wait,
        And watch—and wait!

Oh, strange are the birds and the sheep that dwell
    Here in the land of dreams!
But you must not see, and you must not tell,
    However strange it seems,
Or they'll never let you in again,
And it would not please you, baby, then,
        Just to stand by the gate,
        And watch, and wait,
        And watch—and wait!

BEFORE THE FIRE.

THE winds go riding down the wold,
    And back the forest legions throw;
A winter day the hours has told
    On rosaries of drops of snow.
Through close-drawn blinds the lamplight falls,
    And on a drifted whiteness lies,
While here within these cottage walls
    The flames make stars of baby's eyes.

Rude fingers tap upon the pane
    And entrance at the door demand;
The storm king and his lusty train
    Go rushing o'er the land;
But homes where love a vigil keeps
    Know not that summer ever dies,
Know not that summer even sleeps,
    When flames make stars of baby's eyes.

The father to the mother reads,
    The mother busy at his side;
He reads a tale of noble deeds,
    Of men who for a nation died,
But oft they turn and fondly look
    Upon the hero whom they prize
Beyond the people of the book,
    Where flames make stars of baby's eyes.

Fierce winds may ride across the night,
    And storms prevail o'er flood and field,
But where one lamp throws out its light,
    A happy picture is revealed
Of two, who by the fireside sit,
    And watch the glowing flames, while rise
Quick shadows that around them flit
    And mock the stars in baby's eyes.

OCTOBER.

THE year is getting older, day by day;
　　Last night I heard a fierce wind riding by,
　Rattling my western window, and no ray
Of moon or star illumined the black sky.

Older the year has grown; the wind that came
　　Across the changing world last night to ride,
Passed here a year ago; it is the same
　　That rose before and summer's strength defied.

Ah, it is you, my old, familiar friend
　　October, come to pitch your tents awhile,
Madly descending from the earth's far end
　　Over the farthest seas for many a mile.

Yet your fierce advent and your winds severe
　　Are but the bluster of a friend we love;
Though you are winter's neighbor you bring here
　　Rich gifts, and hang your bluest skies above.

To-morrow you will tame your restless steeds
    And drive the water-freighted clouds away;
Then you will scatter far the wild-flower's seeds
    At intervals throughout a peaceful day.

Still, though your skies may be the summer's own,
    Of all your moods I like the wildest best;
I love the wind and its mad, warring tone,
    Its anger, and its yearning and unrest;

For in man's soul there is an answering mood,
    A passionate storm with wind and driving rain
All through a night—love by dull pain pursued,
    Then days when skies are kind and blue again,—

Blue, but they shed their bitter, biting frost,
    And the sun burns with but a mocking heat,
While ghost-like zephyrs seek for something lost,
    Like followers in the summer's slow retreat.

"IN WINTER I WAS BORN."

IN winter I was born,
So all my years I've loved the frost and snow
And the strong tireless winds that, passing, blow
       A battle note forlorn.

I love the year's long night.
The tumult of great storms, the biting air
Make my heart's summer time, when days are fair
       And yield me true delight.

In winter I was born,
And as I came so let me pass away,
Out from the world on a December day
       When the delaying morn

In the far East shall creep
Last time for me; then let the winds I love
Come from their far-off homes and play above
       The place where I shall sleep.

GOOD NIGHT AND PLEASANT DREAMS.

GOOD-NIGHT and pleasant dreams!
Forgotten all that play-day world of yours,
Kind angels lead you now by distant shores;
    Dear childish hands clasped lightly o'er your breast,
        Dear eyes with lids that keep the dark away,
    What sweet content is now by you possessed!
        I feel your breath against my cheek and say
                Good-night, good-night!
                Good-night and pleasant dreams!

    Good-night and pleasant dreams!
The children's lives so different are from ours,
Is there not made for them a land of flowers,—
    A childhood's land of sleep where they are taken,—
        Where dreams are only dreams of childish toys
    And only sounds of childish voices waken
        The quiet ways, and say to girls and boys
                Good-night, good-night!
                Good-night and pleasant dreams!

Good-night and pleasant dreams!
Go to your quiet land of sleep and dreaming,
Beyond the darkness, passed the stars a-gleaming.
   The plains of your sleep-land are green and fair;
      Out of the night they make a land of morning
   From which is banished even childish care;
      Stay on, sleep on, dear child, the night world scorn-
         ing,—
            Good-night, good-night!
            Good-night and pleasant dreams!

Good-night and pleasant dreams!
Good-bye, and gentle angels guard your sleep,
Good-night, and angels watch above you keep.
   Ah, if we could our childish days prolong—
      If sleep would always come as sweet as this,
   Shielding us from the world of dark and wrong,
      Just by the magic of a mother's kiss,
         And her good-night!
         Good-night and pleasant dreams!

WHERE LOVE WAS NOT.

ONCE in a dream I saw a blackened world
　Hung high in space, by bitter winds o'erblown;
And there no forests were, no flowers grew,
No river flowed, but all was sad and drear.
And on that smoke-encircled sphere there were
No cities full of life; no children spent
Glad hours in play; there, laughter ne'er was heard,
And day was endless day, and night ne'er came
With tired husband seeking home and wife,
And "home" was but a mocking echo there.

And walking o'er that world I met a man,
Or ghost of what was man, wan, staring-eyed,
And bowed as though with age, albeit his locks
Were fair, and seeming youthful was his face;
And unto him I said in question: "Why
This waste and desolation, and where are
The people that once dwelt upon this world?
And slow he made reply: "But yesterday
Did Love remove his court from this drear globe,

Which was as fair a world as ever came
From the Creator's hand, and now, so soon,
That Love is flown has come this awful change—
The cheerlessness, the people dead and gone."

He turned from me, it seemed, and I awoke—
Back in a world that is controlled by Love.

DOWN THE AISLES.

L ONE here in vague cathedral gloom I sit,
Far from the busy city's noise and jar.
Such calm! It seems God might just now have writ
A new, sweet song of peace and whispered it
From star to star.

I almost hear a sacred anthem pealing,
As o'er the quiet aisles I turn my eyes;
It seems I hear soft prayers to heaven stealing
Up rays that lead unto the Light-revealing
In Paradise.

I think: "How oft have feet of mourners led
Down these long aisles where perfect silence reigns!
How oft have heart-uniting words been said
There at the altar, whither flowers were spread
From Love's fair plains!

Yes, Death and Love have hither come and gone,
With slow, sad songs, with anthems glad and free;
And still, without, the world treads on and on
In aisles that lead to darkness—or the Dawn,
O God, and Thee!

RUIN.

THE slowly crumbling wall, the broken gate,
O'er which soft silvery threads of Time are spun;
Through turrets tall, once grim and stern as Fate,
Now unresisted steals the changeless sun.

The eager vines close clasp the pillars round,
As though to hide the signs of their decay;
The cheerless chambers echo with each sound
That enters in where Silence holds her sway.

Upon the ground, with torn and riven crust,
There rests the cuirass of some daring knight,
Enfolding but the cold, unspeaking dust
Of him who nevermore shall lead the fight.

And here the chariot-furrowed roadway lies,
Once trod by armies rich in valorous deeds,
Now haunted by the lonely wind which sighs
And creeps among the dead and tangled weeds.

Ruin and ruins everywhere, but yet,
    In fancy, see the myriad castles tall
Whereon the banners fair of Hope are set,
    Then watch the wreck and ruin of it all!

Forsaken cities far beyond the sea
    Hold not such claim to pity as do those
Grand dwellings youth rears in such majesty
    To crumble and form sepulchres for woes.

O memory! keep and guard your treasures well;
    Contented rest, and, what the past endears,
Unto the ever hopeful future tell,
    And voice your glories through the coming years.

HALF FLIGHTS.

I think it were better that lips should forever be mute
Than flattering the voice should sound, or the speech irres-
    olute.

And better that arrows fly far past the mark, over-shot,
Than but timidly sent they should droop and transfix it not.

The race should be vigorously pushed, though uneven the start,
And always, wherever assigned, let us act well the part,
Let firm be the footstep to tally with firm beat of heart.

But more willing am I forever to steadily plod,
Inspired by a thought that my soul is not linked to a clod,
Than failing in flight, to fall, stricken again to the sod,
And stumble along in the pathway that leads me to God.

A KIND OF MAN.

I like a man who all mean things despises,
A man who has a purpose firm and true;
Who faces every doubt as it arises,
And murmurs not at what he finds to do.

I like a man who shows the noble spirit
Displayed by knights of Arthur's table round;
Who, face to face with life, proves his real merit,
Who has a soul that dwells above the ground;

And yet, one who can understand the worry
Of some chance brother fallen in the road,
And speak to him a kind word 'mid the hurry,
Or lay an easing hand upon his load.

Large hearted, brave-souled men to-day are needed,
Men ready when occasion's doors swing wide;
Grand men to speak the counsel that is heeded,
And men in whom a nation may confide.

The world is wide, and broad its starry arches,
But lagging malcontents it cannot hold;
The way of life to him who upright marches,
Has ending in a far-off street of gold.

TRANSFIGURED.

" A cold, hard man I said," as day by day
    I saw him pass the door, or, brooding, sit
Before his cottage, watching children play
The summer's lingering twilight hours away—
    Ever uncouth and grim, with brows close knit.

Until, one day, a wondrous change took place;
    Upon the door the sign of mourning, and
His child lay dead! But, by what heavenly grace
Did all the hardened lines fade from his face,
Leaving of former self no slightest trace,
    As with sweet Grief he journeyed, hand in hand?

LOVE'S POWER.

WITHIN the palace of a brain
A Thought of Love dwelt all alone,
And there was not another Thought
  That ever dared approach his throne;

Until there came a Thought of Hate,
  Half-crouching to the sacred seat,
But, Thought of Love stretched forth a hand,
  And Thought of Hate died at his feet.

FIRE-HUNTING.

WITH dip and glide a light canoe
    Crept through the waters of the lake;
So softly, lightly creeping through
    That it did not the silence break.

A lantern's penetrating glow
    Burned in the dark a path of light,
And far-off, on its margin, lo!
    A pair of eyes gleamed strangely bright!

The paddling ceased; there fell a hush.
    Then came a ringing rifle-shot—
A plunge into the underbrush—
    Upon the beach a dark blood-clot!

With dip and glide a light canoe
    Crept through the waters of the lake,
So softly, lightly creeping through
    That it did not a ripple make.

"HEARTACHE."

[Lines naming a landscape painted by Mr. Theodore C. Steele, owned by Mr. Louis C. Gibson.]

ALTHOUGH the fields of summer time are dear
    And fair the days of sunshine-flooded hours
We would not always have the summer here,—
        We tire of flowers.

Let come a short October afternoon,
    Or yet a dreary day November sends ;—
A mist hangs o'er the tired earth, and soon
        The night descends.

Like some cowled monk grown weary of the world,
    The evening creeps along in somber guise,
Her face in misty shadows thickly furled
        To hide her eyes.

O heartache of the earth, so near to us
    These barren fields have on a sudden grown!
Cool hand of twilight touch us—tremulous,
        Sick and alone.

O skies of gray, come often in our need!
    Come fall, O mists, efface the marks of tears,—
The lessons of our heartache with us read,
      And soothe our fears!

Dear barren field, we lay our hearts on thine,
    And leafless shrub, we make thy grief our own ;
Come, Spring, and touch our hearts with life divine,
      All heartache flown!

FRIENDSHIP'S SACRAMENT.

WHEN I've partaken of your bread and wine,
  And paused awhile beneath your friendly roof,
Good thoughts and honest purposes are mine,
  Awhile from trivial things I stand aloof.

It is a sacrament of friendship there,
  When I've partaken of your bread and wine;
I feel in touch with all things sweet and fair;
  My pilgrimage is to a true home's shrine.

Like the lost Arab, when his host will bring
  The bit of cake, the salt in friendly sign,
When I've partaken of your bread and wine
  Across my desert rose and lotus spring,

And in my heart there is a genial glow.
  To-night above me starry heavens shine,
Yet out of clouds the brightest stars will grow
  When I've partaken of your bread and wine.

OMAR KHAYYAM.

KING of the wise who, long ago,
    Your tents built in the Persian sand,
Let me your sweet contentment know,
    Here in my vigorous Western land.

Some day, when I shall stand beside
    The grave where you have lain so long—
At Nishapur your body died,
    But your soul lives in tender song—

I'll pour upon your tomb the wine
    Some Western grape has given me;
I'll speak some verse, some flowing line
    Born here, beyond the Western sea.

And may the time be early night
    When torches in the desert glow,
And in dim tents appears a light,
    While sounds the camel's moaning, low.

Then I would be at Nishapur,
　　To stand in reverent pause and be
One happy hour a worshiper,
　　Your grave a Mecca made for me.

Oh, my beloved, I shall taste
　　The grape's blood, as your songs have said,
And pour it on the desert's waste,
　　A tribute to the ghostly dead

Whose spirits hover there, and plan
　　Strange journeys that can never end,
But, in a ghostly caravan,
　　For ages through the past extend.

O, Muezzin, from the Tower of Night,
　　Look you toward the tomb of him
Who yearned in song for greater light
　　And found it at the goblet's brim!

Forget him not, because he keeps
　　Such silence; guard in light and gloom
Until I reach the place he sleeps,
　　With wine to pour upon his tomb.

A DISCOVERY.

[According to a Child.]

I have just discovered what makes bread white,
   And why the loaves are so porous and light.

We plant the seed in fall-time in the ground,
      And all the winter long they grow and grow,
And when the fields and woods are winter-bound,
      The tiny blades are green beneath the snow.

And then in summer-time, when winter's dead,
      The ripened wheat is ground to flour, and so
When that light flour is made up into bread,
      We see within the loaves the winter's snow.

And that is the reason why bread is white,
      And why the loaves are so porous and light !

SONNETS

A MODERN PURITAN.

A S though Priscilla had smoothed out the frown
    She had for all things that were worldly-wise—
    As though she stood again 'neath softer skies
Than on the bleak New England rocks looked down,
And all the sorrows of that time could drown,—
    Thus comes one, unaustere, with kindly eyes,
    Stepping from out the past's dim tapestries,
A Puritan with purity her crown.

Yet, not the shy reserve that marks her ways
    Nor lines of strength denoted in her face
O'er which the sweetest light 'neath heaven plays,
    Compel our love, but traces of the race
That passes down its grandeur to our days,
    Seeking the good and spurning all things base!

THE LAW OF LIFE.

[To Mr. Charles H. Ham, author of "Manual Training".]

"LABOR the law of life," that is your creed;
　　　Once it was true that art meant only grace,
　　　"A pretty flower this is," "a glorious face,"
Men said, and so interpreting, did heed
No higher call than came from shepherd's reed:
　　　The brawny arm was for the warrior's mace,
　　　The supple limb was for the champion's race,
But higher, better things were lost indeed!

Now, in this newer day, what change is wrought!
　　　We know the law of life is labor; so
The hand and mind in unison are taught,
　　　With each the other's ready servant. Lo!
What a grand world will swing beneath the sun
When Heart and Hand and Mind are all in one!

TO EUGENE FIELD IN ENGLAND.

GOOD poet of the city by the lake,
  Critic and satirist I wave a hand
   And send this greeting over sea and land—
That kindest spirits round you tend, and make
Your ready feet to walk in Chaucer's wake,
   And in the paths of Keats and Shelley stand;
   Or where the master of all singers planned
His songs, may your heart inspiration take.

Where Dobson's flowers find root in "paven ground,"
   And Andrew Lang and Walter Pater bide,
I know that there for you a joy is found.
   Cease not your western Pegasus to ride,
And when old book plates and rare volumes bore,
Quit London's fog and dwell with us once more.

DEPENDENCE.

WHEN a kind parent first his children guides
    Into a bit of world they have not seen,
    Though often told about its meadows green,
Or of some evil thing that there abides,
Their father's fearful care each one derides;
    His guarded pace to them seems slow and mean
    Till sudden, they go hurrying back to lean
Against his surer, stronger heart.

                                    The sides
Of mountains where men's daring feet would go
    Alluring are, because no man has trod;
The restful slopes are tempting from below,
    Yet seekers will not in the safe paths plod;
Like the weak children they are taught to know
    That man must always follow after God.

BY SHERIDAN'S GRAVE.

I STOOD upon the heights at Arlington,
  And saw Potomac's waters seaward flowing,
    While all about me, past our human knowing
The soldiers lay—men who that soil had won
From enemies as brave, who would not shun
    The wrath that followed on their whirlwind sowing,
    And there among their graves the flowers were grow-
      ing,
And on Virginia shone the springtime sun.

Here lies the idol of my boyish dreaming,
  Beside the storied river that had known
The camp-fires of a mighty army, gleaming
  Where peace to-day her snowy scarf has thrown.
Sleep, Sheridan, beyond this world of seeming,
  Your spirit guard this valley as its own!

VIKING.

[Written In Du Chaillu's Viking Age.]

WHAT has been stolen from time's jealous hand,—
    A newer Greece washed by the Baltic's tide
    Where fire of Northern genius burned and died;
Where long-dethronèd gods ruled o'er the land
And warriors fought with sword and threatening brand?
    Was it these rugged shores that once defied
    The world as it was known to them and tried
Adventurous keels on many an unknown strand?

Parents of mighty nations, kings of the sea!
    Fair-haired, strong-limbed path-blazers of the deep!
How full a life was theirs, how broad and free,—
    Passing one day Gibraltar's tropic steep,
        Seeking a while some Northern coast and drear,
        Or sailing far to find the Western hemisphere!

VIOLIN.

G ENTLY, beneath her perfect rounded chin,
 The instrument is clasped, as mothers hold
  Across their hearts a much-loved child, to fold
It from the world of misery and sin.
She draws the bow across the strings to win
  To life the tones now soft, now strong and bold,
  (But ever breathing some grand truth untold)
That dormant lie within the violin.

O, mystery of music, wondrous art !
  The sympathetic violin but steals
The loves and hates that dwell within her heart—
  The very hopes, the vague desires she feels—
And at the bow's quick touch they rise and start
  In melody that inmost soul reveals.

WHAT THE BABIES SAY.

WHAT things the babies say are listened to
As if the little heads were brimming o'er
With pretty fancies, such as ne'er before
Took form in human mind—as if they knew
The glories of the world, or false or true.
And with their careless-clutching fingers tore
From Miss Pandora's box the bitter store
(If pleased) and handed out the sweets to you.

O baby lips, whose lispings we repeat,
O baby tongue, so eager in attaining
The power through which your wishes may be
heard;
May you remain forever pure and sweet,
And ne'er in anger move, but uncomplaining,
And ever by the noblest promptings stirred.

SECRETS.

H OW well her many secrets nature keeps
    And never tells to us by word or sign,—
    The hidden source whence comes life-giving wine
Which through the trees in springtime tingling creeps;
The dwelling-place from which the wind low sweeps,
    His stalwart forest legions to align
    With leadership of giant oak or pine—
She tells us not but, brooding silent, sleeps.

So, safely locked within the human heart,
    Are joys and sorrows of the long ago,
As hidden springs from which the sad tears start
    When we scarce know the power that moves their flow;
And we from all the world are set apart
    By precious secrets none may ever know.

BLIND.

A S one who in a cavern underground
   Can hear the jars and murmurings which tell
    That far away a busy people dwell,
Not hearing, only knowing by the sound,
So dwells he in a world by darkness bound;
    He hears and feels, but no dawn can dispell
    The night for him on whom no light e'er fell
With power to drive away the night profound.

But not for aye he walks the realm of night,
    For one day there will break upon his eyes
A flood of rarer, dark o'ercoming light
    Than ever flushed the arch of earthly skies,
And for him dawn a morning wondrous bright
    Within the garden lands of Paradise.

A FANCY.

'NEATH sullen skies the marshalled clouds parade;
    The Autumn wind sighs a weird monotone
      In which I hear, in fancy, softly blown,
The stirring bugle notes that once were played
To mocking echoes in a Southern glade;
      I hear the sentinel's quick challenge tone—
      The noise and stir of war, all backward thrown
Across the gulf that peaceful years have made.

But long ago the clouds of war had spent
    Their fury; sounds of strife no longer fill
The field whereon sweet peace has spread her tent—
    But those same bugle tones are sounding still,
And ringing through the starry firmament,
    Whilst Memory's camp-fires blaze upon the hill.

THOREAU.

A prince he was, yet scorning princely ways,
   A priest of nature, simple and sincere,
      To whom the wild free things were far more dear
Than trammeling honors gathered of the days
That only served to show him some new phase
      In life of flower and tree; whose greatest cheer
      Came when the seasons changed and he would hear
The blue bird's note or see the woods ablaze.

Though joining not in endless race with men,
      And caring not to lift life's heavy load;—
         Of quiet life, of solitude though fond,
I love to read the thoughts traced by his pen,
      And fancy that I walk Marlborough road
         Or rest with him by peaceful Walden pond.

www.ingramcontent.com/pod-product-compliance
Lightning Source LLC
Chambersburg PA
CBHW032144010726
47493CB00008BA/2575

* 9 7 8 3 3 3 7 2 5 0 4 4 7 *